For Clara, again, with love

DK Publishing, Inc.
95 Madison Avenue
New York, New York 10016

Visit us on the World Wide Web at http://www.dk.com

Library of Congress Cataloging-in-Publication Data
Hughes, Shirley.
    The lion and the unicorn / Shirley Hughes. — 1st American ed.
        p. cm.
    A DK Ink book.
    Summary: Lenny, a Jewish boy living in London during the Blitz in
World War II, must adjust to many changes and find the true meaning
of courage when he is evacuated to a large mansion in the English
countryside.
    ISBN 0-7894-2555-6
    1. World War. 1939–1945—England—Juvenile fiction. [1. World
War, 1939–1945—England—Fiction. 2. England—Fiction. 3. Courage–
–Fiction. 4. Jews—England—Fiction.] I. Title.
PZ7.HB7395Li   1998
[Fic]—dc21   98-6499
                                                                      CIP
                                                                      AC

Book design by Simon Davis
The illustrations for this book were watercolor
The text of this book is set in 13.5/18 Caslon 540

Printed in Singapore

First American Edition, 1999
2 4 6 8 10 9 7 5 3 1

Published simultaneously in Great Britain by Random House UK.

THE
LION AND THE
UNICORN

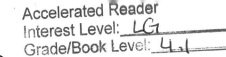

Shirley Hughes

A DK INK BOOK
DK PUBLISHING, INC.

"LONDON's burning,
London's burning!
Fetch the engines,
fetch the engines!
Fire, fire! Fire, fire!
Pour on water,
pour on water!"

Every evening, soon after
dark, the warning sirens
wailed. Then came the
awful droning of enemy
aircraft overhead, and fire-
bombs and explosives
whined and whistled out
of the sky.

LENNY Levi and his mom huddled together under the stairs. Lenny clutched the medal that his dad had given him before he went away. It was made of solid brass: a lion and a unicorn up on their hind legs, fighting each other. Lenny always kept it in his pocket, where he could feel it.

Dad was fighting, too. He was in the army far away while Lenny and Mom clung to each other and longed for daylight.

A unicorn was a mythical beast, Dad had told him. A mysterious, gentle creature. But lions were real, all right.

LIONS stood for being brave. Everybody had to be brave in wartime, not only soldiers but other people, too. Children even. "Be a brave boy, Lenny," Dad had told him when they said good-bye.

Sometimes they got letters from Dad. They came in batches, two or three at a time. Those were the best days. Mom read parts out loud to Lenny while he was having his tea. Dad always put in a drawing for him. Sometimes it was a funny picture like the one of the sergeant. Once he did a beautiful picture of a unicorn with flowers around its neck.

ONE night the bangs
shook the house so badly
that they thought the roof
would fall in. "We should
have gone to the shelter,"
muttered Mom.

Next morning, when they
went out, the Robinsons'
house wasn't there anymore.
Their things were lying all
over the street among the
rubble and broken glass.
The neighbors said that the
Robinsons had gone to the
Rest Center in the night,
wearing blankets.

"That's it!" said Mom.
"We've got to get you out of
here, Lenny."

SOON, suitcase packed and his name on a label pinned to his jacket, clutching his precious medal in his pocket, Lenny joined a crowd of other children at the train station. Mom was there to see him off.

Lenny felt the shape of the lion with his fingertips. He knew he was supposed to be brave. But when he saw so many strange faces he didn't know how to be.

"It'll be a lovely place in the country," Mom told him. "Flowers and rabbits and all that." But she was nearly crying.

LENNY only realized what was really happening when he was in a crowded train. He put his head out the window and shouted, "Don't leave me, Mom! You come with me!"

But the train had already started to move, very slowly at first, then fast gaining speed. "I'll come to see you soon!" called Mom. "Be a good boy." She was a white face among all the others. She shouted something else, but Lenny couldn't hear her. Then she was a tiny figure at the end of the platform, waving and waving.

IT was so dark when at last Lenny arrived that he could not see the place. The windows were blacked out. Then all at once he was in a huge hall, so big that it seemed their whole house in London could have fitted into it easily.

There were no rabbits that Lenny could see. Just some tired grown-ups bustling about, and two girls bigger than him who were called Joyce and Patsy, with a little one called Winnie. They were evacuees. Lenny was one, too.

A lady wearing a great many scarves and woolly cardigans said, "I am Lady De Vass. You must be very tired. Nanny will give you your supper and show you where you are going to sleep."

"We specially asked for girls," Nanny complained, eyeing Lenny.

"I'm afraid it's too late now, Nanny," said Lady De Vass. "And he is not a very big boy," she added kindly.

THE evacuees were to sleep in a big attic room with dark beams overhead. It was chilly and had no electric light or carpets, but there was a nice woody smell. A curtain hung down the middle. Joyce, Patsy, and Winnie were together on one side, and Lenny was alone on the other.

NANNY left a couple of little lamps burning when she said good night. Lenny got down under the blankets. He lay awake for a long time, watching the shadows moving in the high roof. He could hear the girls whispering behind the curtain. Then Winnie began to cry.

Lenny felt numb. The only thing that seemed real at that moment was the brass medal that Dad had given him, underneath his pillow. He went to sleep clutching it.

LENNY woke very early while the girls were still asleep. He could hear faraway stirring noises in the house and faint, echoing footsteps, but no one came. He got out of bed, pattered over to the window, and pulled aside the blackout curtain.

His mouth fell open.

He looked out over a jumble of roofs and chimneys. Not the squat, blackened kind like they had in London, but a fairground of fanciful shapes with grinning gargoyle waterspouts winking in the sun. Beyond that, still wrapped in haze, were gardens, outbuildings, meadows with great spreading trees, and a hill rising behind like a cut-out paper shape.

So this was the country! He had never seen anything like it.

THE great house that Lenny had come to was very old. It had countless rooms. Lady De Vass, who owned the place, lived in one part, Nanny in another. The army of servants who had once looked after the house and garden had now shrunk down to Mrs. B, who cooked; Nelly, who helped with the cleaning and dishes; and an old gardener called Bill Penny.

The evacuees had their breakfast in a kitchen as big as the synagogue Lenny went to at home. It was warm in there, but Lenny was shy and miserable. Nelly smiled at him.

THERE was oatmeal with plenty of milk and thick slices of bread and margarine. But Mrs. B was cross when Lenny would not eat the bacon she gave him.

"There's good food wasted! I'll not have that!" she scolded. "We don't eat bacon in our family," said Lenny in a low voice.

Everyone stopped eating and stared at him. Joyce's eyes were as round and as hard as marbles. Even Winnie stopped whining. Lenny felt his ears turning pink. But he was stubborn. He thought of Mom and Dad, and he still wouldn't eat the bacon. In the end Mrs. B gave in and told the children to take their dirty plates into the scullery and get out from under her feet.

THE girls went off giggling, trailing Winnie after them. Lenny did not know what he was supposed to do, so he wandered off into the yard, through a big gate and into the gardens.

He walked along paths with wide overgrown flower beds and peeped into long greenhouses. He found a goldfish pond like the one in the park at home, but it was choked with weeds and the fish were gone.

THERE was a summerhouse half hidden in ivy, and beyond it, set in a high stone wall, a wooden door.

It was not the door to somebody's house, Lenny knew that. It was a garden door. He remembered hearing somewhere about a secret garden that was locked up for years and years and nobody ever went in.

Cautiously, he pushed the door. It creaked open.

INSIDE was a little garden, like a room without a roof. It had crisscross mossy paths lined with knee-high hedges and stone seats. In the center was a great rosebush with trailers that swept the ground.

It was very quiet in there. Then a bird flew up with a great clatter of wings, and Lenny saw something on the far side of the garden, high up on a pedestal by the wall. At first he thought it was something alive and watching him. But it was too still to be alive. He went over to it.

IT was a unicorn, carved in
stone, just like the one on
his medal. It did not look
fierce. Strong, perhaps, and
very beautiful, with its
curved neck and long mane.
Prancing there alone in the
shadow of the wall, it
seemed as lonely as he was.

Lenny felt relieved to have
found this place. It made
him feel more like himself
again. He made up his mind
to come back whenever he
could.

On Monday morning the evacuees started at the village school. The children were not friendly. They looked at Lenny blankly as though he wasn't there. When the bell rang for morning prayers, Lenny had to stay alone in the classroom, sitting at a desk.

On the playground Joyce, Patsy, and Winnie went off together. Lenny was not included in the boys' soccer game. He stood by the wall until it was time to go home, clutching Dad's medal in his pocket and pretending he didn't care.

On Saturday nights the evacuees had a bath and Nanny inspected their heads for nits. The bath was huge and had iron feet with claws like a lion. They were only allowed four inches of hot water (it was rationed, like almost everything else), and by the time it was Lenny's turn it wasn't even hot anymore.

JOYCE was Nanny's favorite. Nanny curled her hair for her and pressed her hair ribbons for church on Sunday. Joyce put on a special cute voice when she talked to grown-ups, but when the evacuees were on their own she was sharp-tongued and treacherous.

LENNY spent a lot of time wandering alone in the gardens where no one bothered him. One afternoon when he pushed open the door of the walled garden, he found somebody else there. A young man with one leg was sitting on one of the stone benches. He was wearing an old tweed jacket with patched elbows. His empty trouser leg was pinned up and his crutches were propped neatly against the bench beside him.

"Hello there," said the man. "It's all right – I do live here. I was just trying to do a bit of weeding."

"Are you Bill Penny's helper?" Lenny asked him. "Sort of," said the man. "I used to shoot rabbits and pigeons when they got into his vegetable garden, but I don't anymore. This is one of my favorite places."

LENNY hovered by the
gate, not sure what to say
next.

"My name's Mick," the man
continued. "Don't let me
having one leg bother you."
"How did you lose it?"
Lenny wanted to know.
"I left it on a beach in
France," the man told him.
"But I'll be getting a new
one soon."
"Will it be wooden?"
"No, light metal, I think.
With joints."

There was a friendly silence.
Then Lenny remembered
that he was not to talk to
strangers. He was not sure
whether – since this man
lived here – he counted as a
stranger or not, but he
thought he had better be
on the safe side.

"I've got to go now," he said.

Mick just waved.

On wet days Lenny sometimes followed Nelly around the house, and they chatted while she dusted and polished.

In the great hall there was a suit of armor, and swords hanging on the walls, and pictures of battle scenes with soldiers in red coats. There was one full-length portrait of a very grand officer in splendid uniform.

"That's Lady De Vass's grandfather," said Nelly. "They've got a lot of soldiers in the family. Lady De Vass's husband was killed fighting in the First World War and her son's a war hero. He's got medals and all."

"My dad's in the army," Lenny told her.
"I'm joining up myself soon," said Nelly. "Women's Land Army."

LENNY longed for Mom to come, but she wrote to say that she would not visit "until he had settled in." She was working in a firemen's canteen. She was not a good writer, and her letters were short. But she saved up her candy ration and sent Lenny a bar of chocolate now and again.

Lenny saw Mick around the place sometimes, helping Bill Penny or Lady De Vass, but Mick never came into the kitchen for his meals.

"THERE'S something been killing rabbits in my vegetable garden," said Bill one afternoon when he was sipping his tea. "Not that I mind," he added, "I'm glad of it."

"A fox?" suggested Mrs. B.

"No, it's not a fox. More like a big cat. It got some pigeons, too."

"It'll be one of those wild cats that's living in the barn," said Mrs B. "Very fierce, they are."

"Or perhaps a lion escaped from the zoo," said Joyce slyly, looking sideways at Lenny. "Lions kill people. They wait in the dark and spring out at you and tear your stomach out."

THAT night, long after the
others had gone to sleep,
Lenny lay awake, listening
to the night noises outside.
Far away in the dark he
thought he heard a growling,
purring sound, then a shriek
of an animal in pain. He
got up and peeped through
the curtains. Was there
something prowling around?
A black shadow moving
along the hedge?

He hurried back into bed
and pulled the blankets over
his head.

L ENNY thought about Mom and Dad a lot, hoping and hoping they were safe. He longed to see them again.

At school things had gotten a lot worse. The boys had started to shout things at him and make fun of his name.

"Lenny Levi's done a wee-wee!" they jeered. "Wets his bed, don't he?"

LENNY turned hot with anger and shame. It was true about the bed. It was only sometimes, and he didn't think anyone at school knew about it. He guessed that Joyce must have told them.

N<small>ANNY</small> was grim-faced in the mornings when she had to deal with wet sheets. But Nelly found out and came to Lenny's rescue.

"You can beat this, Lenny," she told him. "Everybody does in the end." She smuggled some spare bedding into the attic so that Lenny could put it on before Nanny came in the morning.

SHE whisked away wet sheets and washed them herself. And she lent Lenny her big alarm clock. Lenny set it twice in the night and it went off with a great clang, but the girls never woke up.

The bed-wetting got better. But the boys at school went on teasing.

ONE afternoon Mick came across Lenny sitting hunched on a bench in the walled garden and politely failed to notice his red-rimmed eyes.

"Homesick?" he asked.
At first Lenny was too upset to answer. Then he blurted out all about what the boys at school had said. "It's not even true anymore! Well, hardly at all. But I don't suppose they'll ever stop saying it."

"I used to wet my bed when I was your age," Mick told him. "It was when they sent me away to boarding school."
"Had you done something wrong?" asked Lenny.

"No, they thought it would do me good," said Mick. "My father went there. It was awful. I got teased all the time. Then it started again when I was in the hospital after . . ." He looked down at where his leg had been.

"But you were grown up then!" said Lenny, amazed. "Yes. I cried a lot, too. But I got through it somehow. And so will you, or my name's not Mick De Vass!"

There was a long silence. Lenny stared at Mick. "You're the war hero!" he said at last. "You've got medals for bravery – Nelly told me!"

"I was frightened all the time in the fighting," said Mick. "But I suppose you can't be brave if you're not frightened in the first place. My father was really brave, a fine officer. I am only a private."

"My dad's a private," said Lenny proudly. "He's fighting the Germans, like you did. I've got his medal."

"I never wanted to fight Germans or anyone else," Mick told him. "It's cruelty, bullying, and oppression we're fighting against." Lenny was not quite sure what this meant, but he got the general idea.

"I used to come here to this garden to see the unicorn when I was a boy during the school holidays," said Mick. "I used to long to be brave and manly and all the things they wanted me to be. But there are different kinds of courage. And I'll tell you one thing. The boys who say those things to you haven't got much. None at all, in fact!"

Later, when he was alone, Lenny thought a lot about what Mick had said. Gradually the bed-wetting stopped altogether. Knowing a real war hero who had had the same problem helped. He even forgot about prowling lions.

But then something happened that was much worse.

Mom's weekly letters stopped coming. Every morning Lenny waited anxiously by the gates for the postman to arrive, but there was nothing for him. He told nobody how worried he was. But he started to have bad dreams, about searching for Mom, and running and running, and lions leaping out at him and pinning him down with their terrible teeth and claws.

The bed-wetting started again. In the end everything was just too terrible to be borne.

ONE night Lenny waited
till the girls were asleep. He
had his suitcase already
packed. He put his precious
medal in his pocket and
crept downstairs to the back
kitchen. It was difficult to
unbolt the back door without
making a noise, but he
managed it, standing on a
chair.

He was running away. He
had to get back to London.

HE planned not to go by
the main drive, which went
around the front of the
house, in case he was seen.
Instead he would cut
through the gardens, into the
orchard, through a hole in
the hedge, and across the
field to the road.

There was a bright moon.
Lenny's sharp shadow
tracked him nimbly along
the silent paths.

In the vegetable garden he scampered past raspberry beds and rows of staked-up beans where anyone, or anything, could be hiding.

When he reached the orchard he broke into a run, weaving from one tree trunk to another, crouching low over his suitcase. When he reached the hedge he stopped short.

He thought he heard something moving stealthily and carefully through the grass on the other side. He listened. The whole night seemed to be breathing, purring, growling. He was sure something was coming through the hole in the hedge.

Lenny did not stop to find out what it was. He dropped his suitcase and ran.

Now the dark, many-chimneyed shape of the house seemed to be flying swiftly against the moon, too far away to run to now. But he ran all the same, wildly, until he was heaving for breath. Now he was on the path by the summerhouse. He saw the door to the walled garden. He pushed it open, fell inside, and slammed it shut behind him.

LENNY was crying now, but he felt safe. The garden was completely quiet. The rosebush was frozen in the moonlight. Underneath, in its dense shadow, something glowed softly. It moved gently.

Lenny wasn't frightened. He went toward it. And at that moment he saw the unicorn.

It was alive, glimmering under the rosebush, sitting on its haunches with its one spiraling horn and its long, white, silky mane. It turned its beautiful neck and looked at him.

Lenny knelt down. He laid his head between its hooves with his face in the grass. He was very tired. Almost at once he fell, as though from a great height, into a deep sleep.

HE woke with the sun hot
on his neck. It was morning
and the unicorn had gone.
The statue was in its usual
place, watching over the
garden.

Lenny got up and looked
around. He knew that
something had changed
inside him. It seemed now
that it was his own night
fears that had been chasing
him. He went out of the
garden, closing the door
softly behind him, and
began to walk back to the
house.

THE lion and the unicorn were back inside Lenny's head, and on his medal. But one important thing was real, and that was what the unicorn stood for.

"Different kinds of courage," Mick had said. Now, after last night, Lenny thought he really knew what that meant. Perhaps with his new unicorn courage, he would try to hold on for a while and see if things got better. Anyway, he didn't seem to care much what Joyce and the rest of them said or did anymore. They were only a load of mean, mangy old girls after all.

LENNY came to where the garden met the back drive. As he turned the bend he saw a figure coming toward the house from the opposite direction. A smallish person in a brown coat. A familiar walk. There was a good distance between them. Lenny quickened his pace. Then he broke into a run. Now, as he got closer, the outline of that person was blurred with tears.

LENNY tore the last few yards. "Mom – oh, Mom!" he shouted. And he threw himself into her arms.

"Didn't you get my letter?" said Mom after a while. "Bombed out. A direct hit – the whole house gone. Lucky I was working at the canteen that night."

"I never got no letter," sobbed Lenny.
"The letterbox must have got it," said Mom.
"I was running away," Lenny tried to tell her. "But then..." His voice choked. It was too difficult to explain.

"Lucky you didn't," said Mom, "or we might have missed each other. You're a brave boy, Lenny; a real hero, you are. After you left it seemed like even bombs would have been better than us being separated. But now I've come to take you away. We're going to your auntie Rachel's in Wales. It's by the sea, Lenny. And guess what – your dad's coming home on leave! We'd better go and tell them."

Lenny felt in his pocket to check that his medal was safe. So he, Lenny Levi, was brave after all. He knew that didn't mean he would never be scared again. But at that moment, he felt he could face anything.

Jaunty now, and hand in hand with Mom, he walked toward the house.